MARVEL
GUARDIANS OF THE GALAXY

MARVEL

GUARDIANS OF THE GALAXY

BASED ON THE TV SERIES WRITTEN BY
STEVE MELCHING, MATT WAYNE, MAIRGHREAD SCOTT & DAVID McDERMOTT

DIRECTED BY
JAMES YANG & JEFF WAMESTER

ANIMATION ART PRODUCED BY
MARVEL ANIMATION STUDIOS

ADAPTED BY
JOE CARAMAGNA

SPECIAL THANKS TO
HANNAH MACDONALD & PRODUCT FACTORY

EDITORS
MARK BASSO & CHRISTINA HARRINGTON

SENIOR EDITOR
MARK PANICCIA

COLLECTION EDITOR: **JENNIFER GRÜNWALD**
ASSOCIATE EDITOR: **SARAH BRUNSTAD**
EDITOR, SPECIAL PROJECTS: **MARK D. BEAZLEY**
VP PRODUCTION & SPECIAL PROJECTS: **JEFF YOUNGQUIST**
SVP PRINT, SALES & MARKETING: **DAVID GABRIEL**
HEAD OF MARVEL TELEVISION: **JEPH LOEB**

EDITOR IN CHIEF: **AXEL ALONSO**
CHIEF CREATIVE OFFICER: **JOE QUESADA**
PUBLISHER: **DAN BUCKLEY**
EXECUTIVE PRODUCER: **ALAN FINE**

MARVEL UNIVERSE GUARDIANS OF THE GALAXY VOL. 3. Contains material originally published in magazine form as MARVEL UNIVERSE GUARDIANS OF THE GALAXY #9-12. First printing 2016. ISBN# 978-0-7851-9914-4. Published by MARVEL WORLDWIDE, INC., a subsidiary of MARVEL ENTERTAINMENT, LLC. OFFICE OF PUBLICATION: 135 West 50th Street, New York, NY 10020. Copyright © 2016 MARVEL No similarity between any of the names, characters, persons, and/or institutions in this magazine with those of any living or dead person or institution is intended, and any such similarity which may exist is purely coincidental. **Printed in the U.S.A.** ALAN FINE, President, Marvel Entertainment; DAN BUCKLEY, President, TV, Publishing & Brand Management; JOE QUESADA, Chief Creative Officer; TOM BREVOORT, SVP of Publishing; DAVID BOGART, SVP of Business Affairs & Operations, Publishing & Partnership; C.B. CEBULSKI, VP of Brand Management & Development, Asia; DAVID GABRIEL, SVP of Sales & Marketing, Publishing; JEFF YOUNGQUIST, VP of Production & Special Projects; DAN CARR, Executive Director of Publishing Technology; ALEX MORALES, Director of Publishing Operations; SUSAN CRESPI, Production Manager; STAN LEE, Chairman Emeritus. For information regarding advertising in Marvel Comics or on Marvel.com, please contact Vit DeBellis, Integrated Sales Manager, at vdebellis@marvel.com. For **Marvel** subscription inquiries, please call 888-511-5480. Manufactured between 9/16/2016 and 10/24/2016 by SHERIDAN, CHELSEA, MI, USA.

9 BASED ON **"WE ARE FAMILY"**

MARVEL

GUARDIANS OF THE GALAXY

ROCKET

GROOT

DRAX THE DESTROYER

GAMORA

PETER QUILL, A.K.A. STAR-LORD

PREVIOUSLY:

The Guardians came into possession of a mysterious Spartaxan cube that holds a map to an object of immense power called the Cosmic Seed. Half Spartaxan, Star-Lord is the only one able to access the map. Now the Guardians must find the Seed before Thanos does.

PLANET GRUCKKUK.
"ACCORDING TO THE ENERGY READINGS IN THESE GEMS, THE COSMIC SEED WAS HERE...BUT ISN'T ANYMORE."
"ANOTHER DUD, QUILL? ARE YOU SURE THE MAP IN YOUR CRYPTO CUBE EVEN WORKS?"
WELL, I'M NOT LEAVING EMPTY-HANDED.
IF SOMEONE'S STRIP MINING THESE ROCKS, THEY COULD BE WORTH SOMETHING.
WE CAN CASH THEM IN FOR UNITS AND CALL OFF THIS WILD GOOSE CHASE ONCE AND FOR ALL.
AND LET THE COSMIC SEED AND ITS LIFE-GIVING POWERS FALL INTO THE HANDS OF THANOS, ROCKET?
AND MISS MY OPPORTUNITY TO EXACT MY REVENGE ON THANOS FOR WHAT HE HAS DONE TO MY FAMILY?
LIKE YOU'RE THE ONLY ONE WHO'S LOST HIS FAMILY, DRAX? YOU DON'T SEE ME GETTIN' ALL TEARY-EYED ABOUT IT.
SUBJECT 89P-13, SUBJECT 272-99--
--YOU ARE ORDERED TO SURRENDER IMMEDIATELY!
I AM GROOT!
I NEVER THOUGHT I'D HEAR THOSE NAMES AGAIN!
OR SEE THOSE KRUTACKIN' TIN CANS!

FRIENDS OF YOURS, ROCKET?
WHAT IS SUBJECT 89P-13?
DO I LOOK LIKE I HAVE ANY FRIENDS?
ZAM!
A BLAST FROM MY PAST--
--BUT I'M BLASTING BACK!
BADOOM
WAY TO GO, ROCKET! YOUR LASER CANNON COLLAPSED THE MINE!
RUN!

WE SEEM TO BE OUT OF LAND TO RUN ON!
GAH!

SPLASH
SPLASH
SPLASH

SUBJECT 89P-13, YOU WILL SURRENDER--
--AND RETURN TO HALFWORLD WHERE YOU BELONG.
LET ME GO!
I WON'T BE YOUR LAB RAT! NOT AGAIN!
DRAX, CAN'T YOU SWIM EVEN A LITTLE?
WATER IS FOR COWARDS. LIKE FISH.
WE'VE GOT OTHER THINGS TO WORRY ABOUT--
--THOSE ROBO-GOONS ARE MAKING OFF WITH ROCKET AND GROOT!
GET TO THE MILANO--WE HAVE TO FOLLOW THEM!
VRSSH!

HALFWORLD.
"SUBJECT 89P-13, SUBJECT 272-99-- WE HAVE BEEN TRACKING YOU FOR SOME TIME VIA YOUR CYBERNETIC IMPLANTS.
"YOU HAVE INFORMATION WE REQUIRE."
YOU WERE ARRESTED FOR SABOTAGING OUR MINING OPERATIONS ON PLANET GRUCKKUK...
...DESTROYING OUR SUPPLY OF RARE MINERALS WITH UNUSUAL PROPERTIES.
UNUSUAL?
THE COSMIC SEED POWER! ITS ENERGY WAS ALL OVER THOSE GEMS!
THE MINERALS HAVE PROVEN TO BE A MORE EFFICIENT MEANS OF ACCELERATING EVOLUTION THAN THE KIND OF CYBERNETIC EXPERIMENTS WE USED TO ENHANCE YOUR INTELLIGENCE.
UNFORTUNATELY, THAT HAS ALSO ENABLED THE SUBJECTS TO REBEL.
YOU WILL TELL ME THE LOCATION OF THEIR REBEL BASE OR SUFFER THE CONSEQUENCES.
I DON'T KNOW NOTHIN' ABOUT NO REBEL BASE. BUT EVEN IF I DID...
...I WOULD NEVER TELL YOU VACUUM CLEANERS!
WE ANTICIPATED THAT YOU WOULD FEEL THAT WAY...
...SO WE PREPARED A CONTINGENCY PLAN.
JEN?
MOM?!
Y-YOU'RE STILL HERE...AND YOU'RE WALKING UPRIGHT NOW?

I'M SURPRISED YOU EVEN RECOGNIZE ME AND YOUR SISTER, RUNT. YOU HAVEN'T RETURNED SINCE YOU RAN OFF WITH THIS TREE!
I AM GROOT!
YOU LOOK LIKE A BAD SEED TO ME.
MY NAME'S ROCKET NOW, MA. NOT "RUNT."
I THINK I LIKED IT BETTER WHEN YOU ONLY CHITTERED.
BUT IT'S GOOD TO SEE YOU BOTH.
AWW, MY BOY!

ZZZZRRRRKKKK
ENOUGH CHATTER, RODENTS!

ALL RIGHT! ALL RIGHT. YOU WIN.
THE INFORMATION YOU WANT IS IN THAT STORAGE-DIMENSION VIAL THAT YOU STOLE FROM MY POCKET.

HMMMM

VRRT!
WAIT A SEC, THAT'S NOT THE LOCATION OF THE REBEL BASE--

--IT'S MY BLASTER!
CATCH!

ZAPPA!
MY BAD!
ZAPPA! ZAPPA!

I AM GROOT!
BOOM!
ZAPPA!
KRASH!

C'MON! WE'RE BUSTIN' OUTTA HERE!

FREEZE!
I AM GROOT?

RANGER?
YES, IT'S ME, MOM! DUCK!

ZARK! ZARK!
ZARK!

WELL IF IT ISN'T THE GOLDEN BOY.
IT'S GOOD TO SEE YOU AGAIN, RUNT.

THIS IS MY TEAM-- WAL RUS AND BLACKJACK O'HARE!
I KNEW YOU'D COME RESCUE US, RANGER!
WE'D BETTER SCOOT, BOSS. THERE COULD BE MORE OF 'EM!

I AM GROOT?
MY BROTHER. HE ALWAYS HAD A KNACK FOR SHOWING UP TO CLAIM THE REWARD AFTER THE REAL WORK WAS ALREADY DONE.

LATER.
THIS IS YOUR REBEL BASE?

THIS IS THE PLACE WHERE THEY EXPERIMENTED ON ME!

THE ROBOTS MADE TOO MANY OF US TOO SMART. WE EVENTUALLY TOOK UP ARMS AND DROVE THEM OUT.

I AM... GROOT?
SUSPICIOUS? SEEMS LIKE JUSTICE TO ME!
LET'S CALL THE OTHER GUARDIANS TO PICK US UP SO WE CAN DITCH THIS JOINT--FOR GOOD THIS TIME!

FORGET IT, BRO. ALL COMMUNICATION SIGNALS BOUNCE OFF THE GALACIAN WALL THE ROBOTS BUILT AROUND THE PLANET.
WHAT'S YOUR HURRY, ANYWAY?

NOW THAT WE'RE REUNITED...
...LET'S SAVOR THE MOMENT.

WOULD IT KILL YA TO SMILE, RUNT?
SO OUR CONQUERING HEROES HAVE ARRIVED!

PYKO, THIS IS MY BROTHER RUN--ERR... ROCKET. AND HIS FRIEND, GROOT.
PYKO IS THE SUPER-EVOLVED GENIUS WHO MADE OUR REVOLUTION POSSIBLE.
THEY COULDN'T SUPER-EVOLVE YOUR EYESIGHT?
OW! OW! OW! WHAT DID I DO, MA?!
IN ALL YOUR SPACE ADVENTURES YOU NEVER LEARNED TO RESPECT YOUR ELDERS?
WELL, IF YA DON'T MIND, IT'S BEEN A LONG DAY AND ME AN' GROOT ARE GONNA GRAB SOME GRUB.
LONG LIVE THE REVOLUTION, AND ALL THAT JAZZ.

ARE YOU HAPPY? I LOST 'EM.
NOW WE CAN SNOOP AROUND A LITTLE IF THAT'LL MAKE YOU FEEL BETTER, MR. SUSPICIOUS.
EW. THIS PLACE IS JUST AS SPOOKY AS IT WAS THE LAST TIME WE WERE HERE.
I CAN ALMOST HEAR THE VOICE OF THAT CREEPY LAB CHIEF.
SUBJECT 89P-13, HELP ME!
GAH!
I-IT'S YOU! WHAT HAVE THEY DONE TO YOU?
HELP ME. PYKO AND HIS REBELS HAVE FUSED ME IN MY DOCKING STATION.
IT LOOKS LIKE YOU GOT WHAT YOU DESERVED!
YOU ARE RIGHT TO HAVE THOSE FEELINGS. BUT WE SOUGHT ONLY TO IMPROVE ANIMAL LIFE IN THE NAME OF SCIENCE. OUR INITIAL ATTEMPTS WERE... CRUDE, BUT WE HAVE SINCE SEEN THE ERROR OF OUR WAYS.
WE FOUND A MINERAL ON THE PLANET GRUCKKUK THAT ACCELERATED THE NATURAL PROCESS OF EVOLUTION, WHICH WE WERE HOPING TO USE TO UNDO OUR EXPERIMENTS, BUT IT WAS TOO LATE, AND PYKO STARTED A REVOLUTION.
PLEASE, SUBJECT 89P-13, YOU MUST HELP ME. WHAT WE DID WAS WRONG...
...BUT WHAT PYKO WANTS TO DO IS SO MUCH WORSE.

I SEE YOU FOUND OUR OLD FRIEND THE LAB CHIEF. THAT CRUMB!
THE LAB CHIEF WAS A LOT OF THINGS, BUT I NEVER KNEW HER TO BE A LIAR. SO TELL ME--
--WHAT'S REALLY GOING ON HERE?
THE NEXT STEP IN EVOLUTION!
WHICH WE WILL DEMONSTRATE FOR YOU. BUT FIRST--
--YOU HAVE SOMETHING WE WANT.
DID YOU THINK WE WOULDN'T FIND OUT YOU WERE HIDING THIS MINERAL FROM US, RUNT?
HEY!
THANK YOU, RANGER. AND AS YOUR REWARD--
VRRRT
--YOU GET TO BE THE FIRST AMONG US TO BE ENLIGHTENED!
NO! RANGER! DON'T DO IT!
RRRRRRR--

--ROARR!
SOON ALL THE ROBOTS WILL BE DESTROYED, AND THIS PLANET WILL BE OURS! AND THEN...
...SO WILL THE GALAXY!
WE WILL NEVER BE VICTIMS AGAIN!
MOM'S NOT GONNA LIKE THIS!
RANGER--
BRKOOM!
--DESTROY THE TRAITORS!
SORRY TO DO THIS TO YOU, BRO...
...BUT I'VE GOTTA GET MOM AND SIS OUT OF THIS MADHOUSE!
ZARK!
GROOT, NOW!

GET THE MINERAL!
KRSSH!
I AM GROOT?
NO!
WHAM!
I AM GROOT?
HALF OF THE MINERAL IS BETTER THAN NOTHING! LET'S GO!

BUT WHERE ARE WE GOING?
IS THAT ANY WAY TO TALK TO YOUR MOTHER?
JUST GET ON THE BIKE! HURRY!

IS--IS THAT RANGER?
ROARRR!
NOT ANYMORE.

LET THEM GO. HALF OF THE MINERAL IS ALL WE NEED.
THE ROBOTS CAN'T STOP US NOW!

I GOTTA BE NUTS TO WALK BACK INTO A PRISON I JUST BROKE OUT OF!

HALT, SUBJECTS!
SUBJECTS WILL DROP THEIR WEAPONS.
SETTLE DOWN, YOU MOOKS. I COME IN PEACE.
THE LAB CHIEF SAID YOU HAVE A WAY TO REVERSE PYKO'S EVOLUTIONARY PROCESS?

AFFIRMATIVE. BUT WE REQUIRE AT LEAST A SMALL SAMPLE OF THE MINERAL, WHICH WE NO LONGER POSSESS.
THEN TODAY'S YOUR LUCKY DAY. HAND IT OVER, GROOT.
THERE THEY ARE!

ALL RIGHT, JERK-BOTS! RELEASE MY FRIENDS, NOW!
RELAX, QUILL. THE BOTS ARE ON OUR SIDE NOW.
I'LL EXPLAIN LATER.

THESE ARE THE KINDA LOSERS YOU'RE HANGING AROUND WITH THESE DAYS, RUNT?
NOT IN FRONT OF MY FRIENDS, MA!
"MA"?! YOU'RE ROCKET'S MOTHER?!

I CAN'T WAIT TO MEET THE REST OF YOUR FAMILY--
UHH... WHAT'S THAT?
THAT...

...IS MY BROTHER... AND HIS BAND OF EVOLUTIONARIES!
ROARRR!
ROARRR!
I AM GROOT!

ROARRR!
YOW! THAT EASTER NIGHTMARE I HAD AS A KID IS COMING TRUE!

YOU EVER FIGHT A WALRUS BEFORE?
WHAT'S A WALRUS?

MOM, SIS-- I'M GETTIN' YOU OUTTA HERE!

IT'S PYKO!
VRRRR!

KEEP *GOING,* MA! *I'LL* TAKE CARE OF HIM!

NOBODY MESSES WITH MY FAMILY!
ESPECIALLY NOT SOME *NEAR-SIGHTED REPTILE!*
YOU WILL NOT UNDO MY WORK!

HOW ABOUT I UNDO YOUR RIDE?

SMELL YA LATER, WRINKLED PUSS!

SUBJECT 89P-13, THE DEVOLUTION DEVICE IS ONLINE--

BOOOM!

WHAT'VE I DONE?! I CRASHED PYKO RIGHT INTO THE *DEVOLUTION DEVICE!*
CRASH!
BASH!

SUBJECT 89P-13, I REQUIRE ASSISTANCE...

THE DEVICE I WAS CARRYING IS DAMAGED, BUT STILL OPERATIONAL. IT MAY, HOWEVER, HAVE JUST ENOUGH POWER FOR A SINGLE SHOT.
IF YOU AIM THE RAY TOWARDS THE SKY, IT WILL REFLECT OFF OF THE GALACIAN WALL THAT SURROUNDS THE PLANET.
BUT THEN EVERY ENHANCED CREATURE WILL BE HIT BY THE DEVOLUTION RAY, INCLUDING ME AND MY FAMILY.
BUT IT'S THE ONLY WAY TO PUT AN END TO PYKO AND HIS EXPERIMENTS ONCE AND FOR ALL!

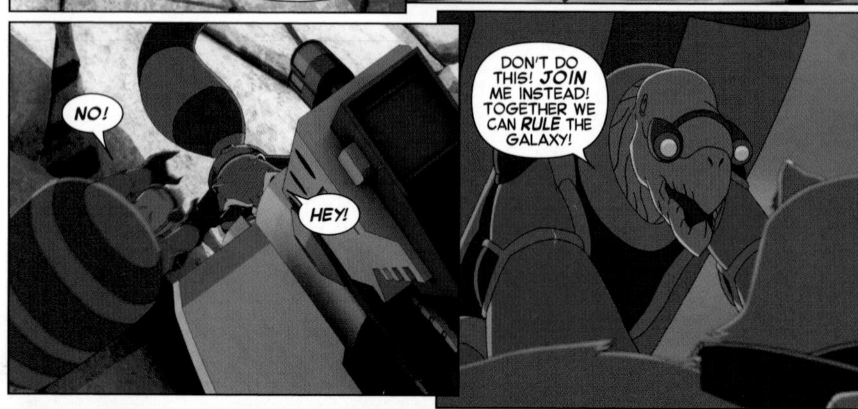
NO!
HEY!
DON'T DO THIS! JOIN ME INSTEAD! TOGETHER WE CAN RULE THE GALAXY!

I'M NOT INTERESTED IN RULING THE GALAXY, YOU SHRIVELED-UP MANIAC!
I'M HERE TO GUARD IT!

TALKING AND WALKING UPRIGHT WAS FUN WHILE IT LASTED--
CLICK

--BUT I'VE GOT A WORLD TO SAVE!
VMMMM!

I-IT'S GONE! ALL OF MY WORK, IT'S...
...IT'S... GONE...
AWW! YOU'RE JUST AN ITTY-BITTY BUNNY WABBIT!
RANGER! YOU'RE BACK!
LISTEN, MA...BEFORE WE ALL REVERT BACK TO WOODLAND CREATURES, I JUST WANNA SAY...
...IN A WAY I'VE NEVER BEEN ABLE TO TELL YOU BEFORE...IN WORDS...
...I LOVE YOU.
AND I LOVE YOU, TOO...
...ROCKET.
HERE WE GO!

SOMETHIN' AIN'T RIGHT...
WHY DIDN'T I CHANGE BACK, TOO?
YOU WERE EVOLVED USING AN OLDER, CYBER-NETIC METHOD. THE DEVOLUTION RAY HAS NO EFFECT ON YOU.
IT'S LIKE YOU ALWAYS SAY--THERE AIN'T NO THING LIKE YOU, EXCEPT YOU.
YEAH...
GOODBYE, MA.
AGAIN.
THEY WILL BE SAFE. NOW THAT WE UNDERSTAND THE ERROR OF OUR WAYS, WE WILL PROTECT ALL ANIMAL LIFE ON HALFWORLD.
YOU BETTER...

"...OR I'LL COME BACK AND REPROGRAM YOU ALL!"
I'M SORRY YOU LOST YOUR FAMILY AGAIN. I KNOW WHAT THAT'S LIKE.
EH, FAMILIES ARE OVERRATED ANYWAY.
BUT STILL...
"...THEY SEEMED PRETTY GREAT."
YEAH. THEY ARE, AREN'T THEY?
THE END.

QUILL, IF I DON'T GET OFF OF THIS SHIP SOON, I'M GONNA TEAR MY FUR OUT! WE'VE BEEN FOLLOWING YOUR MAP TO THE COSMIC SEED FOR THREE DAYS NOW--
--WHERE IS THIS DEAD MOON WE'RE LOOKING FOR?
HOLD ON TO YOUR TAIL, ROCKET. WE'RE COMING UP ON IT NOW.
ARE YOU SURE ABOUT THAT, GENIUS?
ATMOSPHERE, WATER, VEGETATION-- DO YOU EVEN KNOW WHAT A "DEAD MOON" IS? THIS AIN'T IT!

THE (SUPPOSEDLY) DEAD MOON OF MANDALA.
THE STAR MAP IN MY CRYPTO-CUBE SAYS IT IS, AND THE MAP KNOWS ALL.
LIKE IT HASN'T STEERED US WRONG BEFORE.

WE'VE SEEN THAT THE SEED ACCELERATES LIFE--
--SO MAYBE, JUST MAYBE, IT CAN BRING A MOON BACK FROM THE DEAD.
THE SEED IS HERE, I KNOW IT.
HEY! WATCH IT, GROOT!
I AM GROOT!
ROCKET, YOU SAID THAT GROOT GREW OUT OF THE CLUMSINESS HE HAD AS A SAPLING--
WHUMP!
UHH... HEY, GUYS? WAS THIS GIANT TREE STANDING IN OUR WAY JUST A SECOND AGO?
RRRRRR... RRRRR...
ROCKET? ARE YOU ALL RIGHT?

ANNOYING RODENT!
I WILL ROAST YOU OVER A FLAME AND FEAST UPON YOUR CARCASS TO CELEBRATE MY VICTORY IN THE ARENA THIS DAY!
GRR--

WHOA! ISN'T THAT A BIT HARSH, DRAX?
WHY IS EVERYONE ACTING LIKE THEIR OLD SELVES?
HRR--

RRAAGH! RRRRR!
OW!
WHAT DID YOU BITE ME FOR, FLEA BAG? I'M YOUR FRIEND!

I HAVE NO FRIENDS, RAVAGER!
ACK! GAMORA!

I AM LOYAL ONLY TO THANOS!

THAT DOES IT, I'M PUTTING YOU ALL IN A TIME-OUT!
FROOSH!
ICE?
KRKKK!
IT SEEMED TO ME THAT SOMETHING ABOUT THIS PLANET'S SURFACE WAS SUCKING THE MATURITY OUT OF ALL OF YOU.
HOW COME YOU WEREN'T AFFECTED, QUILL?
BECAUSE STAR-LORD HAS NO MATURITY TO BEGIN WITH.
NO FREEZE ME! MANDALA WANTS TO PLAY!
THE PLANET--IT SPEAKS!
AND WITH THE VOICE OF A CHILD!
LOOK, KID-- PLANET, WHATEVER-- WE'RE NOT HERE TO PLAY.
WE'RE HERE TO FIND THE COSMIC SEED, THEN WE'LL BE ON OUR WAY.

NO! STAY! PLAY WITH MANDALA!
HE'S BREAKING THE ICE!
KSSH
KSSH
KSSH

RESIST THE REGRESSION, GAMORA. DON'T GO ALL FIGHTER MODE ON ME AGAIN.

I--I DON'T WANT TO HURT YOU...

...I WANT TO ANNIHILATE YOU ALL!
VRSSSH!
HUH?
IT'S NEBULA'S SHIP!
VRSSSH!

MY SISTER?
I THOUGHT SHE WAS DESTROYED, BUT I GUESS NOT.* SHE'S PROBABLY HERE FOR THE COSMIC SEED JUST LIKE WE ARE.
*NEBULA'S SHIP WAS THOUGHT TO BE DESTROYED AT PLANET SARAWAT IN ISSUE #7!
I DO NOT KNOW WHAT THIS "COSMIC SEED" IS, BUT I WILL NOT ALLOW NEBULA TO GET HER HANDS ON IT BEFORE I DO.
IF THIS "COSMIC SEED" IS A PRIZE WORTH FIGHTING FOR, YOU WILL BOTH HAVE TO GET THROUGH ME TO GET IT!
THE COSMIC SEED IS AN OBJECT OF IMMEASURABLE POWER THAT BAD GUYS WANT TO TURN INTO A WEAPON.
AND WE'RE NOT GONNA FIND IT IF YOU'RE STANDING HERE REVERTING TO YOUR OLD SELVES!
OR ARE WE? MAYBE NOT IF THEY'RE STANDIN HERE...BUT IF I CAN GET THEM MOVING...
HEY, LOSERS! IF YOU WANT TO GET THE COSMIC SEED, YOU'LL HAVE TO FIGHT ME FOR IT!
COME AND GET ME, KRUTACKERS!

ELSEWHERE.
YOU CAME BACK, LIKE YOU PROMISED!
NOW YOU CAN PLAY WITH MANDALA'S NEW FRIENDS!
THE GUARDIANS ARE NO FRIENDS.
I'VE RETURNED TO THIS PRIMORDIAL ARMPIT BECAUSE I BURIED SOMETHING EARLIER TO FEED ON YOUR NEWFOUND LIFE-GIVING ENERGY.
LET ME SHOW YOU!
OW! YOU HURT MANDALA!
KRAKOW!
RISE, AND LET US SHOW THOSE WHO THOUGHT WE HAD BEEN DEFEATED--
--AAAH!
--THAT RONAN THE ACCUSER LIVES ONCE MORE!

WHAT IS THIS PLACE? WHO DARES TO DISTURB RONAN?

LORD RONAN, IT IS I, NEBULA. YOUR LOYAL AGENT.
NEBULA...?

PERHAPS YOUR UNIVERSAL WEAPON WILL JOG YOUR MEMORY.
THEN WE WILL OVERTHROW THANOS AND RULE THIS UNIVERSE TOGETHER!

I--I DO NOT REMEMBER YOU...
...BUT I REMEMBER THAT RONAN THE ACCUSER SHARES POWER WITH NO ONE!
"SLOWING DOWN ALREADY?"

COME GET ME!
NEENER, NEENER, POO POO!
WE WILL TEAR YOU LIMB FROM LIMB!
OH BOY.
COME ON, SLOWPOKES! I'M RIGHT HERE!
WHAT IS THIS DISTURBANCE?
IS THERE NO PEACE FOR RONAN THE ACCUSER?
FIRST NEBULA AND NOW RONAN'S ALIVE, TOO?!
YOU'VE GOT TO BE KIDDING ME.

GAMORA, WHO IS THIS SCUM IN YOUR COMPANY?
YOU REMEMBER HER, BUT NOT ME?
JEALOUSY ISN'T A GOOD LOOK FOR YOU, NEBULA.
LORD RONAN, I BRING YOU THIS INSOLENT RAVAGER WHO CLAIMS TO HAVE DESTROYED YOU.
TECHNICALLY, IT WAS ALL OF US WHO DESTROYED HIM.
YAY! NOW THAT WE'RE ALL TOGETHER, WE CAN PLAY!
A KREE ACCUSER DOES NOT "PLAY."
WRMMM
GAH!

THAT'S IT! NOW YOU'RE GONNA MAKE ME MAD!
GET 'IM, DRAX!
I HAVE NO QUARREL WITH HIM.
YOU DID! ER, YOU WILL! AND SINCE WHEN DO YOU NEED AN EXCUSE TO BEAT THE SNOT OUT OF SOMEBODY?
GAMORA'S WEAK, LORD--
IF YOU WISH, I WILL DESTROY THEM FOR YOU, LORD RONAN.
--LET ME PROVE MYSELF TO YOU!
SINCE YOU INSIST ON A FIGHT, I WILL OBLIGE!
BUT THERE'S NO NEED TO ARGUE--
HNN!
--I CAN FIGHT YOU BOTH AT THE SAME TIME!
WUDD!
GAH!

YOO-HOO! THE BAD GUY'S OVER THERE!
CAN WE STOP FIGHTING EACH OTHER AND GO AFTER RONAN, PLEASE?
WSSSH!
WSSSH!
ENOUGH! YOU FOOLS ARE NOT WORTHY OF MY TIME!
KRAKK!
WHAT DID YOU DO TO MANDALA?
KRAKK!

I AM GROOT!
WHAT THE--?!
KRKKK!

IF YOU WILL NOT BOW TO ME...
HNN!
...THEN YOU SHALL PERISH!
AHHH!
HE'S TRYING TO BURY US ALIVE!
GAMORA! REMEMBER WHO YOU ARE! YOU'RE A GUARDIAN NOW, YOU'RE ONE OF US!
PLEASE, HELP ME UP!
I WOULD NEVER JOIN THE LIKES OF YOU, RAVAGER--
UNNF!
THINK AGAIN, SISTER!
SMAK!

AAAAHHHHHHHHHH!

I'VE GOT YOU!
MY ANKLE ROCKETS AREN'T JUST GOOD FOR TRAVELING, THEY CAN ALSO CUSHION A--
CRMMM!
--FALL!
YOU SAVED MY LIFE. WH-WHY?
BECAUSE THAT'S WHAT FRIENDS DO.
MAYBE YOU DON'T REMEMBER, BUT WE ARE FRIENDS. ALL OF US.
NOW, EITHER WE ACT LIKE IT AND GET BACK TO GROUND LEVEL, OR THAT CREEP UP THERE WITH THE HAMMER'S GONNA TAKE THE COSMIC SEED AND RULE THE UNIVERSE.
GROOT, STRETCH YOUR ARMS OUT--
SKRRTCH

"--WE'RE GONNA NEED 'EM!"
I AM GROOT!
THIS IS MORE LIKE IT! TEAMWORK!
SHUNK!
I AM GROOT!
YOU'RE DOING FINE, GROOT. YOU MAY HAVE BEEN CLUMSY IN YOUR EARLY YEARS, BUT TRUST ME, YOU GREW OUT OF IT.
I WILL COOPERATE FOR NOW, BUT WHEN OUR COMMON ENEMY HAS BEEN DEFEATED, I WILL SLAY YOU ALL!
AND YOU GREW OUT OF THAT, GAMORA.
THE FOG HAS PASSED. MY MIND IS CLEAR. I REMEMBER NOW WHAT I AM TASKED TO DO--
--AND THIS MOON HAS JUST THE POWER I NEED TO OBLITERATE THE ANCIENT ENEMIES OF MY PEOPLE.
MANDALA--

KRAKK!
--TAKE ME TO XANDAR, THE HOME PLANET OF THE NOVA CORPS, AND I WILL ALLOW YOU TO SERVE ME!

THIS GAME IS NO FUN!

SOMETHING FEELS... FUNNY.
I DO NOT SEE THE HUMOR IN THIS SITUATION.
THE PLANET IS MOVING! SHIFTING IN SPACE!

MANDALA DON'T WANT TO GO TO XANDAR, BUT BAD GUY MAKE ME!
MANDALA, WE CAN HELP YOU, BUT ONLY IF YOU LET MY TEAM GO BACK TO THEIR NORMAL SELVES.
OKAY, MANDALA DO WHAT FRIEND ASK.

GROOT, SEE IF YOU CAN BREAK RONAN'S HOLD ON HIM!

I AM GROOT!

ARGH!
YOUR PLANT CREATURE IS RELEASING MY GRIP!
RNNK!
RONAN THE ACCUSER IS ALIVE?
WELCOME BACK TO REALITY, ROCKET. NOW, GET HIM!
IF YOU REVERTED TO YOUR OLD SELF, HOW ARE THE GUARDIANS STILL ALIVE?
WELL...

...I GREW UP.
WAKK!

IT IS WORKING! FRIEND GROOT IS FREEING MANDALA FROM RONAN!
MANDALA CAN GO BACK TO MANDALA'S HOME AWAY FROM XANDAR!
KEEP IT UP, GROOT! DIG THOSE ROOTS DEEP!
I AM GROOT!
NO! RELEASE MANDALA NOW!
WSSH!
SHUNK!
I AM GROOT?
NO MERE PLANET CAN STAND UP TO MY UNIVERSAL WEAPON!
MANDALA BELONGS TO ME!

XANDAR HAS BEEN FOUND GUILTY BY RONAN THE ACCUSER!

LET THIS MOON SERVE AS AN INSTRUMENT OF JUSTICE TO DELIVER THE PUNISHMENT!
MANDALA DON'T LIKE THIS GAME!
MANDALA NO NEED GROOT TO FIGHT MANDALA'S BATTLES--

--MANDALA FIGHT FOR HIMSELF!
BAD PEOPLE MUST LEAVE MANDALA--
--NOW!
KROOM!
AAHH!

ARGH!

MANDALA FEEL MUCH BETTER NOW, THANKS TO FRIENDS!
I WISH I COULD SAY THE SAME. RONAN STILL LIVES, WHICH MEANS HE HAS NOT FACED JUSTICE FOR WHAT HE HAS DONE TO MY FAMILY.
WHAT DO YOU MEAN? MANDALA JUST TOSSED HIM INTO SPACE.
HE ALWAYS SURVIVES, ONE WAY OR ANOTHER.
ACCORDING TO MY CRYPTO-CUBE, THE COSMIC SEED WAS HERE TO BRING MANDALA AND RONAN TO LIFE...BUT NOW IT'S GONE AGAIN.

SO OUR SEARCH CONTINUES.
WHERE ARE MANDALA'S FRIENDS GOING?
SORRY WE CAN'T STICK AROUND AND PLAY, MANDALA, BUT WE'VE GOT A GALAXY TO PROTECT.

BUT MANDALA WANT TO PROTECT THE GALAXY, TOO!
WE COULD ALWAYS USE A BIG, STRONG PLANETOID IN OUR RANKS...HOW WOULD YOU LIKE TO BE AN HONORARY MEMBER OF OUR TEAM?
MANDALA LIKES NEW FRIENDS.
YOU KNOW, MANDALA--YOU'RE PRETTY COOL YOURSELF.
THE END.

THE GRANDMASTER
VS
THE COLLECTOR

ROCKET, FLY US OUT OF THIS GRAVITY STORM BEFORE THE PRESSURE CRUSHES MY SHIP INTO SCRAP LIKE IT DID THESE OTHER SHIPS!
WHAT DO YOU THINK I'M DOING, QUILL?
HOLD ON TO YOUR KRUTACKIN' HIDES!
WHEW! MADE IT BACK OUT! AM I AN AWESOME PILOT OR WHAT?
BUT ACCORDING TO MY STAR MAP, THE COSMIC SEED IS ON THE OTHER SIDE OF THAT STORM.
IF WE DON'T FIND THE SEED BEFORE THANOS DOES, HE'LL USE ITS POWER TO CONQUER THE GALAXY!
THERE'S GOTTA BE SOME WAY TO FLY THROUGH IT!
THE ONLY WAY TO FLY THROUGH A GRAVITY STORM IS WITH A REPULSOR FIELD GENERATOR. THE ONLY PLACE YOU COULD MAYBE FIND SUCH A THING IS ON--
OHHH NO.
OH, YES! SET A COURSE--

"--WE'RE GOING TO KNOWHERE!"
HEY, COSMO, WHAT'S SHAKIN'? BESIDES YOUR TAIL, THAT IS.
DA, DA, IS GOOD JOKE BECAUSE COSMO IS DOG.
BUT IN SERIOUS, COSMO KNOW THAT PETER QUILL--WHO IS ALSO KNOWN AS STAR-LORD--COME TO KNOWHERE FOR REPULSOR FIELD GENERATOR TO GET THROUGH GRAVITY STORM.
STOP READING MINDS, YA MUTT. IT'S CREEPY.
DO YOU KNOW WHERE I CAN FIND ONE?
IS ONE PERSON IN KNOWHERE WITH FIELD GENERATOR. UNFORTUNATELY--
C.C.C.P
THAT PERSON IS ME.
JUST OUR LUCK--

--THE COLLECTOR!
THE LAST TIME I SAW YOU QUILL, YOU DESTROYED MY COLLECTION*--
*SEE ISSUE #3.
--AND NOW YOU SEEK MY HELP?
NO, IT'S NOT LIKE THAT! I'M NOT LOOKING FOR A FAVOR...I'M HERE TO DO BUSINESS.
WELL, THE GENERATOR IS NOT FOR SALE. BUT IF YOU ARE INTERESTED IN A TRADE...
"...THERE IS ONE TASK I HAVE BEEN LOATH TO UNDERTAKE."
SHMMM!
EW. WHAT REEKS?!
MOOMBAS. THEY ARE A GIFT FOR MY BROTHER.
TRANSPORT THESE MOOMBAS TO THE GRANDMASTER ON CONJUNCTION, AND THE GENERATOR IS YOURS.
BUT MOOMBAS CANNOT BE TRUSTED!
AS A YOUNG WARRIOR, I WAS ATTACKED BY A MOOMBA HERD.
NOT MY PROBLEM, DRAX.
OH, BEFORE I FORGET--DO NOT FEED THE MOOMBAS ANYTHING BUT GRASS UNTIL YOU ARRIVE AT CONJUNCTION, OR THINGS COULD GET...MESSY.
"MESSY"?
YEESH! IS THIS JOB WORTH IT, QUILL?
LEAVE THAT TO ME.
HEY, COLLECTOR...

LATER...
KRSSH! SMASH!
ROCKET, WHAT'S ALL THE RUCKUS DOWN THERE?

WHY DID YOU EVER AGREE TO THIS CRAZY SCHEME, QUILL?
BECAUSE THE COLLECTOR ALSO THREW IN THIS COOL COWBOY HAT.
THE MOOMBAS ARE GETTING AWAY!
"AWAY"? WHAT DO YOU MEAN?

THEY'RE GETTING OUT!
OH, NO.

WHAT ARE THEY DOING?
I TOLD YOU MOOMBAS CANNOT BE TRUSTED, QUILL--

--THEY ARE TELEPORTING US AWAY!
THEY CAN DO THAT?
IT'S ALWAYS BEEN SAID THAT MOOMBAS TRAVEL VAST DISTANCES, BUT I DIDN'T KNOW THAT'S HOW THEY DID IT.
ACCORDING TO THESE COORDINATES, WE'RE A THOUSAND LIGHT-YEARS CLOSER TO CONJUNCTION.
THEY APPEAR TO BE HEADED TO THAT MOON, QUILL.
"THEN SO ARE WE, GAMORA."
ALL MY LIFE I'VE DREAMED OF BEING A COWBOY, BUT I NEVER IMAGINED I'D BE HERDING SPACE COWS.

WHAT'S SO GREAT ABOUT SITTING IN THE DIRT AROUND A HEAT SOURCE?
BECAUSE THIS SOURCE OF HEAT HAS HELPED TO PREPARE OUR GRAND FEAST.
WHO'S READY TO EAT?
LATER. FIRST, LET'S JOIN IN THAT OLD EARTH TRADITION OF SINGING AROUND THE CAMPFIRE!
WHERE DID YOU GET THAT MUSICAL INSTRUMENT?
IT CAME WITH THE HAT.
I WORKED HARD ON THIS MEAL--
--FIRST YOU EAT, THEN YOU SING!
GULP! OKAY, OKAY!
SLURP!
HRMFF!
'SCUSE ME!
ROCKET, YOU WILL RECEIVE THE HONOR OF THE SECOND BOWL!
DO I HAVE TO?

BOY, DRAX, THIS LOOKS DELICIOUS--
OH, LOOK! WHAT'S THAT UP THERE?!
HUH?
SPATCH!
ROCKET, THE COLLECTOR SAID THE MOOMBAS CAN ONLY EAT GRASS!
SO? WHAT COULD POSSIBLY HAPPEN?
PTOO!
CHOMP CHOMP
CHOMP
BOOM!
EXPLOSIVE SPIT!
I DIDN'T SEE THAT COMING!
TO THE MILANO!
PTOO!
BOOM!

BLLLRRRRRFFF!
GAH! THAT TASTED LIKE AN OLD SHOE...WITH AN OLD FOOT STILL INSIDE!
SNORT
HELLO. WHAT'S THAT YOU GOT AROUND YOUR NECK THERE, PARTNER?
INSIDE...
CHECK THIS OUT--ACCORDING TO THIS BIOSCAN, THE MOOMBAS HAVE BEEN INJECTED WITH AN EXPLOSIVE COMPOUND, BUT IT ONLY REACTS TO CERTAIN KINDS OF PROTEIN.
IF THEY DON'T EAT MEAT, THEY HAVE NO PROBLEM--
--BUT IF THEY DO, THE MOOMBAS CAN GO BOOMBAS--AND BLOW UP A SMALL MOON.
OR A PLANETOID LIKE CONJUNCTION.
LOOK AT WHAT I TOOK OFF OF THE ALPHA.

DEET!
GREETINGS, DEAR BROTHER! OR...WHATEVER IS LEFT OF YOU.
I JUST WANT TO SAY--
--I WIN!
THE COLLECTOR WAS USING US TO BLOW UP HIS BROTHER-- EVEN IF IT MEANT BLOWING US UP, TOO.
YOU'RE SURPRISED?
AT LEAST WE FOUND OUT BEFORE THE MOOMBAS COULD DO ANY DAMAGE. LET'S GET OUT OF HERE.
AND LEAVE THEM HERE TO BLOW THIS MOON OUT OF THE GALAXY? NO...
...WE NEED TO HERD THEM INTO SPACE WHERE THEY WON'T DO AS MUCH DAMAGE.
I WILL MONITOR THE PERIMETER FROM THE SHIP. ENSURE THAT NO ONE--
ZKAM!
I'M HIT!
BUT BY WHO?!
ZKAM!

WELL, WELL, IF IT AIN'T MY FAVORITE TERRAN AND HIS PACK OF MISFITS.
YONDU?!
DON'T YOU WORRY YOUR LITTLE HEAD, ME AND MY RAVAGERS AREN'T HERE FOR YOU, LADY--
"--WE'RE HERE FOR YOUR MOOMBAS!"
THEY MAY SEEM UNCONTROLLABLE, BUT IF YOU KNOW WHAT THEY'RE DOING--
--YOU CAN GET THEM TO FOLLOW YOU ANYWHERE!
WHAT? NO, YONDU! DON'T!

THOSE MOOMBAS ARE RIGGED TO EXPLODE!
I KNOW. THE COLLECTOR AND THE GRANDMASTER HAVE BEEN FUEDING FOR YEARS. THAT'S WHY THE GRANDMASTER HIRED US TO TAKE THESE CREATURES BACK TO KNOWHERE AND BLOW THE COLLECTOR UP INSTEAD!
IF YOU'RE GONNA BLOW UP KNOWHERE--
--YOU'LL HAVE TO BLOW ME UP WITH IT.
IN THAT CASE, I'M GONNA MISS YOU, BOYO.
WHOA! SLOW DOWN--
--YOU MADE ME LOSE MY HAT!
CURSE YOU, FOUL MOOMBAS! I SWEAR TO YOU, PETER QUILL WILL BE AVENGED!

SNORT
A MOOMBA! YONDU LEFT ONE BEHIND!
STAND BACK BEFORE IT--
SLLURP!
EWW! IT'S A FRIENDLY.
THERE'S NO SUCH THING AS A FRIENDLY MOOMBA!
SPTOO!
BOOM!
I AM GROOT!
WHAT DO YOU MEAN "MAKE AN ANTIDOTE." ANTIDOTES DON'T GROW ON TREES--
HMM. OR DO THEY?
"FIRST, WE'LL NEED SOME INDREDIENTS FROM DRAX'S KITCHEN..."
NOW, WE JUST ADD A BIT OF THIS, AND...
OKAY, BIG GUY-- STICK YOUR FEET IN HERE AND LET'S SEE WHAT GROWS.
I AM GROOT!
NO, BUDDY-- YOU DID IT!

CHOMP
THAT'S A GIRL! EAT IT UP.

TAKE COVER!
PTOO!
SPLASH!
IT WORKED!
I CAN'T BELIEVE I'M HAPPY THAT SOMETHING DIDN'T BLOW UP!

WE CAN USE THIS MOOMBA TO CREATE A PORTAL THAT TAKES US TO THE OTHERS SO THEY CAN EAT THE FLOWERS ON GROOT'S HEAD, TOO.

THIS ISN'T RIGHT...
HUH?
I AM DRAX THE DESTROYER. WHAT KIND OF WARRIOR WOULD I BE IF I LET INNOCENTS PERISH BECAUSE OF MY FEAR OF MOOMBAS?
LET ME RIDE.

KNOWHERE.
VMMM
WE'RE HERE! UNLESS I DO SOMETHING, KNOWHERE IS DOOMED!
WHA--? THAT'S NOT MY ELEMENT BLASTER! I MUST'VE DROPPED IT WITH MY HAT!
NOW WHAT AM I GONNA DO?
VVV--
DO NOT FRET, STAR-LORD! THE CAVALRY HAS ARRIVED!
--VMMMMM

RAVAGERS, GET THAT STRAY MOOMBA!

FIRST YOU WILL HAVE TO *CATCH* THIS MOOMBA!
ZARK!
ZARK!
DRAX! I'M LOSIN' MY--

--GRIP!
AAAH!
I AM GROOT!
HUH?
PAFT!
THANKS FOR THE SAVE, GROOT!
I AM GROOT!

HOLD STILL, QUILL!
THIS ISN'T WHAT IT LOOKS LIKE, GAMORA!
IT LOOKS LIKE YOU'RE BEING DRAGGED BY A MOOMBA.

SLIKK!
OOOKAY, THEN IT'S EXACTLY WHAT IT LOOKS LIKE.

FASTEN YOUR SEAT BELT, GROOT. WE'RE GOIN' UPSIDE DOWN--

--'CAUSE DINNER IS SERVED!
CHOMP
CHOMP
CHOMP

FORGET SOMETHING?
MY ELEMENT BLASTER! BUT WHAT ABOUT MY HAT?
YOU'LL HAVE TO TAKE THAT UP WITH DRAX.

FREEZE!
WHAT'S THIS NOW?

THE FIRST PERSON TO MOVE A MUSCLE GETS BLASTED BACK TO THEIR HOME PLANET...
...SO COMMANDS RHOMANN DEY OF THE NOVA CORPS!

AM I GLAD TO SEE YOU! ME AND MY COHORTS WERE JUST TRYING TO RETURN THESE STOLEN ANIMALS BACK TO THEIR RIGHTFUL OWNER AND THESE SCRUFFY NE'ER-DO-WELLS ATTACKED US!

CORPSMAN DEY!
CORPSMAN DEY, WHAT YONDU SAYS IS NOT TRUE.

WELL, THE PART ABOUT RETURNINK STOLEN ANIMALS, COSMO MEAN.
THE GUARDIANS WERE TRANSPORTINK MOOMBAS BY REQUEST OF RIGHTFUL OWNER...THE COLLECTOR!

MISTER COLLECTOR? IT APPEARS THAT I'VE FOUND A DOZEN OF YOUR MOOMBAS--WHICH HAPPEN TO BE ILLEGAL TO OWN.
WHAT DO YOU HAVE TO SAY FOR YOURSELF?
MY MOOMBAS? MOOMBAS MAY BE RARE, BUT NOT QUITE RARE ENOUGH TO PIQUE MY INTEREST, CORPSMAN.

PTOO!

OH, NO! WE DIDN'T GET TO FEED THEM ALL YET!
EXPLOSIVE MOOMBA SPIT AT FOUR O'CLOCK!
GET CLEAR!

BA-BOOM!

I'M HIT!

HECK, I AIN'T ONE TO LOOK A GIFT GETAWAY IN THE MOUTH...

...RAVAGERS, LET'S GO!

CORPSMEN, FOLLOW THOSE RAVAGERS! DON'T LET THEM GET AWAY!
NOW'S OUR CHANCE TO GET AWAY! HERD THE MOOMBAS AND LET'S GO!
THE MOOMBAS? WHAT DO YOU WANT THEM FOR?
OH...
"...YOU'LL SEE."
VMMMMM
PRETTY GENIUS OF ME, ISN'T IT?
OUR NEW PETS TELEPORTED US THROUGH THE GRAVITY STORM. NOW, ASSUMING THE STAR MAP IS ACTUALLY RIGHT THIS TIME...
...LET'S GO FIND US THE COSMIC SEED.

LATER...
I DON'T BELIEVE IT. ANOTHER DUD? YOUR MAP STINKS!
IT'S NOT THE MAP'S FAULT WE GOT HERE TOO LATE AND THE COSMIC SEED IS ON THE MOVE AGAIN.
AT LEAST IT'S TELLING US WHERE TO GO NEXT.

IT'S NOT A COMPLETE LOSS-- THE NOW NON-EXPLOSIVE MOOMBAS SEEM HAPPY. THERE'S PLENTY OF GRASS FOR THEM TO GRAZE--AND NO ONE TO HURT.

SLURP!
IT WILL MAKE A FINE HOME FOR THEM.
YOU MEAN...

...THEY'RE NOT COMING WITH US?

I AM GROOT?
SNIFF OF COURSE I'M NOT CRYING!
SNIFF

SURE.
AND I AM NOT CRYING EITHER.
SNIFF
THE END!

SO, THE PITCHER ROWS THE LL, AND THE BATTER HITS IT.
UNLESS THE BATTER MISSES THE BALL--THAT'S CALLED A STRIKE.
HE MILANO. OME OF THE UARDIANS OF HE GALAXY.
UNLESS IT'S A BAD PITCH, THEN IT'S A BALL-- I MEAN THE BALL IS ALWAYS CALLED A BALL, BUT--
HOW HAVE NONE OF YOU EVER HEARD OF BASEBALL? B-A-S-E-B-A-L--!
ZOMPF!
WHAT THE...?
IS-- IS THAT A DOG?
A TELEPORTING DOG?
'SCUSE ME, BUT THAT'S MY CRYPTO CUBE YOU'RE SNIFFING AROUND!
THAT IS THE UGLIEST FLERKEN I'VE EVER SEEN.
WHAT IS A "DOG"?
I'M GONNA HAVE TO ASK YOU TO GET AWAY FROM IT, POOCH.
HERE! FETCH!

OH, GOOD. HE DIDN'T RUIN IT WITH HIS SLOBBER.
THIS CUBE HOLDS THE STAR MAP TO THE COSMIC SEED. IF THANOS FINDS THE SEED BEFORE WE DO, HE'LL USE ITS POWER TO CONQUER THE UNIVERSE.
ZOMPF!

PANT! PANT!

QUILL, LOOK OUT!

ZOMPF!
I AM GROOT?
THAT TELEPORTING FURBALL TELEPORTED GAMORA AND STAR-LORD OUTTA HERE!
BUT TO WHERE?
I DON'T KNOW, DRAX...
...BUT WE'RE GONNA FIND OUT!

COME BACK HERE WITH MY BASEBALL!
FORGET YOUR ALL, QUILL, WE NEED TO IGURE OUT HOW TO GET ACK TO THE MILANO!
WHOA, WHAT IS THIS PLACE?
DO YOU THINK THE DOG WAS TRYING TO LEAD US HERE ALL ALONG?
WHAT IS IT, BOY? DID TIMMY FALL DOWN A WELL?
ON EARTH, THAT JOKE IS HILARIOUS, BY THE WAY.
OKAY, I'LL BITE. LET'S SEE WHAT'S IN THIS POD.
IT'S--IT'S A SLEEPING PRINCESS! LIKE IN A FAIRY TALE--
WHAM!
DO NOT DARE LAY YOUR FOUL HANDS ON MEDUSA, QUEEN OF THE INHUMANS!
I WASN'T GONNA!
EW! DID YOU GRAB ME WITH YOUR HAIR? GROSS!

HAIR?!
UHN!
WHO SENT YOU? ARE YOU KREE?
NO ONE SENT US! YOUR WALKING SOFA OVER THERE BOARDED OUR SHIP AND TELEPORTED US HERE!
LOCKJAW, IS THAT TRUE?

"YOU BROUGHT THESE TRANGERS HERE TO ATTILAN?"
THE BEACON IN UILL'S HELMET DS HERE, IN THIS FLOATING CITY...
...BUT THERE DOESN'T SEEM TO BE ANYTHING HERE BUT THESE WORTHLESS STATUES.
THE "WORTHLESS STATUES" ARE ATTACKING!
I AM GROOT!
I'M NOT APOLOGIZING TO THESE HUNKS OF ROCK!
ALPHA PRIMITIVES-- CEASE THIS ATTACK!
SORRY FOR THE MISUNDERSTANDING. I WAS EXPECTING SOMEONE ELSE.
I AM MAXIMUS, SUPREME LEADER OF THE INHUMANS.
WHAT ARE "INHUMANS"?
EARTHLINGS, ACTUALLY.
THOUSANDS OF YEARS AGO, THE KREE EXPERIMENTED ON A TRIBE OF PREHISTORIC HUMANS, MAKING THEM GENETICALLY SUPERIOR TO THEIR BRETHREN.
MY ANCIENT ANCESTORS WERE FEARED AND HATED, FORCED TO LIVE IN SECLUSION IN THIS MARVELOUS CITY OF ATTILAN.
"DID YOU SAY YOU'RE FROM EARTH?"

THEN HOW DO YOU DO THAT THING WITH YOUR HAIR?
PROLONGED EXPOSURE TO TERRIGEN CRYSTALS IN THE CAVERNS BENEATH THIS CITY HAS GIVEN US EACH UNIQUE AND AMAZING POWERS.
BUT THEN THE PLAGUE APPEARED.
PLAGUE?!
IT ONLY AFFECTS INHUMANS. IT SLOWLY TURNS OUR BODIES INTO TERRIGEN CRYSTAL.

AT THE URGING OF MY HUSBAND, WE PLACED OURSELVES IN STASIS AND LAUNCHED OUR CITY INTO SPACE, HOPING SOMEONE WOULD FIND AND CURE US--

MY HUSBAND! THE KING IS MISSING! AND SO IS HIS BROTHER, MAXIMUS!
LOCKJAW--

"--TELEPORT US TO MAXIMUS' LAB RIGHT AWAY!"
YOU'VE SEEN THE EFFECT OF THE PLAGUE ON OUR SERVANT CLASS, THE ALPHA PRIMITIVES--THEY'RE INDESTRUCTIBLE.

BUT FOR THE RULING CLASS, THE PLAGUE IS QUITE DEADLY. THAT'S WHY, AFTER YEARS OF TIRELESS WORK I HAVE FOUND A CURE.

BUT I'M AFRAID THE REST OF THE ROYAL FAMILY--LIKE MY BROTHER BLACK BOLT--MAY BE TOO FAR GONE TO EVEN ATTEMPT TO CURE HIM.
MAXIMUS!

WHAT HAVE YOU DONE TO YOUR KING?
ROCKET? DRAX? YOU FOLLOWED US HERE?
MY KING? BY RIGHTS, I SHOULD BE THE KING!
I ISOLATED THE TERRIGEN PLAGUE! I FOUND THE CURE! ALL WHILE "MY KING" DID NOTHING. SAID NOTHING.
YOU KNOW THAT BLACK BOLT CANNOT SAY ANYTHING. HIS POWER IS IN HIS VOICE--EVEN HIS SLIGHTEST WHISPER CAN LEVEL ENTIRE PLANETS!
THAT IS BUT ONE OF HIS STRENGTHS, WHICH BRINGS US TO MY BEST INVENTION YET--
--A HELMET THAT GRANTS ME COMPLETE AND TOTAL CONTROL OF MY BROTHER'S MIND.
BLACK BOLT, DESTROY THEM ALL!
NO...

I AM GROOT!
FWIK!
I AM GROOO--
CRASH!
GAMORA, WAIT! WE NEED A PLAN--
WHAMMM!
OR YOU CAN JUST IGNORE ME AND DO YOUR OWN THING, AS USUAL!

I'M WARNING YOU--DON'T MAKE ME OPEN THIS BOX! THERE'S A WEAPON INSIDE THAT CAN WIPE OUT THE WHOLE CITY!

YES! DO IT! THIS I MUST SEE! PLEASE!
OOOKAY... BUT YOU ASKED FOR IT.
POW! BRIGHT LIGHT IN YOUR EYES!
AAHHH!
B-BLACK BOLT...?
MY DEAR HUSBAND, IT'S NOT YOUR FAULT--YOU WEREN'T UNDER YOUR OWN CONTROL--
--BUT MAXIMUS' HOLD ON YOUR MIND HAS BEEN BROKEN--AT LEAST TEMPORARILY.

IT LOOKS LIKE MAXIMUS FLEW THE COOP.
LET'S GET THIS MIND CONTROL DOOHICKEY OFF HIS MAJESTY'S HEAD WHILE WE HAVE THE CHANCE--
DON'T TOUCH IT! HIS ANTENNA HELPS HIM FOCUS HIS ENERGY ON STAYING SILENT, SO HE DOESN'T ACCIDENTALLY DO HARM.
AND THE PLAGUE IS EVEN WORSE THAN BEFORE WE WENT INTO STASIS.
THE COSMIC SEED ENERGY FROM THE CRYPTO CUBE MUST HAVE ACCELERATED ITS GROWTH.
THAT'S...
...AWESOME.
I DO NOT THINK THAT WORD MEANS WHAT YOU THINK IT MEANS.
NO, DRAX, IF COSMIC SEED ENERGY MADE THE PLAGUE WORSE, THEN TAKING THE ENERGY AWAY SHOULD MAKE IT BETTER!
AND MY CUBE ABSORBS COSMIC SEED ENERGY!
SEE?!

HMM. BUT IT'S NOT TAKING ALL OF THE PLAGUE AWAY. THERE MUST BE ANOTHER SOURCE OF COSMIC SEED ENERGY SOMEWHERE IN ATTILAN.
MAYBE THE COSMIC SEED'S RIGHT UNDER OUR FEET!
IF YOU'RE WRONG, THIS IS JUST ANOTHER COSMIC SEED WILD GRUBLOG CHASE.
AND IF I'M RIGHT, ALL WE NEED IS TO PUT THE COSMIC SEED INTO THE CUBE WHERE IT BELONGS AND BOOM--NO MORE PLAGUE!
WE'VE NEVER EVEN SEEN THE COSMIC SEED--WE HAVE NO IDEA HOW IT WOULD REACT TO BEING PUT BACK IN THE CUBE.
WHY DOESN'T ANYONE EVER LISTEN TO ME?
IF YOU DON'T WANT TO LOOK FOR THE SEED WITH ME, THEN FINE--

"--I'LL FIND IT MYSELF."
OH, HEY, KING SILENT-BUT-DEADLY--I SAID I CAN DO THIS ON MY OWN.
WHAT? WHAT IS IT?
STAR-LORD. THIS IS A PLEASANT SURPRISE.
I TOLD YOU I WAS EXPECTING SOMEONE ELSE--RONAN THE ACCUSER!
MAXIMUS, WHAT HAVE YOU DONE?
IN EXCHANGE FOR AN INVINCIBLE CRYSTAL ARMY, ATTILAN BECOMES PART OF THE KREE EMPIRE--
--WITH ME AS THE SUPREME LEADER, OF COURSE.
BUT RONAN'S AN OUTLAW EVEN AMONG HIS OWN PEOPLE!
YOU CUT A DEAL WITH THE ONE PERSON IN THE UNIVERSE WHO'S CRAZIER THAN YOU, MAXIMUS.
ALPHA PRIMITIVES, ATTACK!

SO, YOU ARE THE FORMER RULER OF THIS REALM.
YOU CANNOT HOPE TO OVERPOWER MY UNIVERSAL WEAPON...
...EVEN IF YOUR PLAGUE HADN'T ALREADY WEAKENED YOU.
HEY! GIMME BACK THAT HELMET!
THE HELMET BELONGS TO ME.
BY DIVINE RIGHT, I PROCLAIM MYSELF--
--MAXIMUS THE MAGNIFICENT! SUPREME RULER OF THE INHUMANS!

ACCUSER RONAN, I HEREBY SWEAR ETERNAL LOYALTY AND FEALTY TO THE KREE EMPIRE.
YOU PROMISED ME AN INVINCIBLE ARMY, YET YOU PRESENT ME WITH THESE ABOMINATIONS?
I WANT YOU OUT OF MY SIGHT.
BUT... WE HAD A DEAL!
AS ACCUSER OF THE KREE EMPIRE, I DECLARE THAT THIS VILE CITY BE CLEANSED...
...AND YOU WILL SUFFER FOR DECEIVING ME!
AGH! THE PAIN!
ZZZKT!
THIS BELONGS TO ME NOW.
BLACK BOLT, ORDER YOUR PET TO TELEPORT YOU TO THE TERRIGEN CRYSTAL CHAMBER BENEATH THE CITY--

--AND TAKE PETER QUILL WITH YOU.
WHAT'D I DO?
ZOMPF!

AT LONG LAST, THE CRYPTO CUBE IS MINE!
AND SOON, SO WILL BE THE COSMIC SEED.

VMMM!
AS SOON AS MY SHIP REACHES A SAFE DISTANCE, I WILL ORDER BLACK BOLT TO SCREAM--

--AND RID THE UNIVERSE OF ATTILAN--AND THE GUARDIANS OF THE GALAXY--FOREVER.

MAXIMUS, PLEASE--IF YOU GIVE BLACK BOLT THE CURE TO THE TERRIGEN PLAGUE--
--PERHAPS HE'LL REGAIN ENOUGH STRENGTH TO FIGHT OFF THE MIND CONTROL!
YOU MEAN... THIS?
NEVER! IF I CANNOT BE KING, THEN NO ONE CAN!
I WOULD RATHER BE VAPORIZED THAN BOW TO MY BROTHER AGAIN!
SKRASSH!
ALPHA PRIMITIVES, DO NOT ALLOW MEDUSA AND HER FRIENDS TO INTERFERE WITH RONAN'S PLANS!
THIS HAS GONE ON LONG ENOUGH, MAXIMUS!

THE CAVERNS BENEATH ATTILAN.
THE SEED'S NOT HERE EITHER!

BLACK BOLT, THIS IS RONAN THE ACCUSER.
I OWE STAR-LORD A DANCE-OFF--

--SO MAKE HIM DANCE.
ACTUALLY, HEH, I'M NOT REALLY UP FOR DANCING RIGHT NOW.
AND, YOU'RE A SICK MAN, REMEMBER? YOU SHOULD PROBABLY REST.

RONAN'S SHIP.
THIS SHOULD BE FAR ENOUGH.
NOW, BLACK BOLT--

--SCREAM.

DON'T DO IT, BLACK BOLT--
--YOU CAN FIGHT THIS!

IF YOU HAVE TO SCREAM, WHY NOT HAVE LOCKJAW TAKE YOU FAR AWAY FROM HERE WHERE YOU CAN'T HURT ANYONE?
WHAT DO YOU THINK, LOCKJAW?

ZOMPF!
UHH, LOCKJAW?

ZOMPF!
HUH?
GRAB

ZOMPF!

THUNK!
MY CRYPTO CUBE!

YOU SENT LOCKJAW TO FETCH IT! YOU ARE FIGHTING RONAN'S CONTROL!

NOW I CAN ABSORB THE COSMIC SEED ENERGY FROM THE TERRIGEN CRYSTALS AND CURE THE PLAGUE! BRILLIANT!

KRRRK!
THE PLAGUE--IT'S GONE!
WE ARE CURED!
THANKS TO ME AND MY CRYPTO CUBE!
AND LOCKJAW AND BLACK BOLT TOO, I GUESS.
BUT SOMETHING'S WRONG. EVERY OTHER TIME THE CRYPTO CUBE ABSORBED COSMIC SEED ENERGY, IT SHOWED US A NEW COORDINATE ON THE STAR MAP.
THIS TIME THERE'S NOTHING.

WHAT DIFFERENCE DOES IT MAKE? AS SOON AS WE LEAVE ATTILAN TO GO ANYWHERE, RONAN WILL BE OUT THERE WAITING.

LEAVE THAT TO US.
DO WHAT YOU MUST, HUSBAND.

RONAN'S SHIP.
WHAT IS HAPPENING?!
WHY ISN'T ATTILAN ANNIHILATED BY NOW? IT'S--
YOU! BUT YOU SHOULD BE UNDER MY CONTROL, DOING MY BIDDING!
NEVER.
BRMMM!
NOOO!
YOU INHUMANS HAVE NOT HEARD THE LAST OF RONAN THE ACCUSER!
NEITHER YOU, NOR THE GUARDIANS OF THE GALAXY!
THE END!

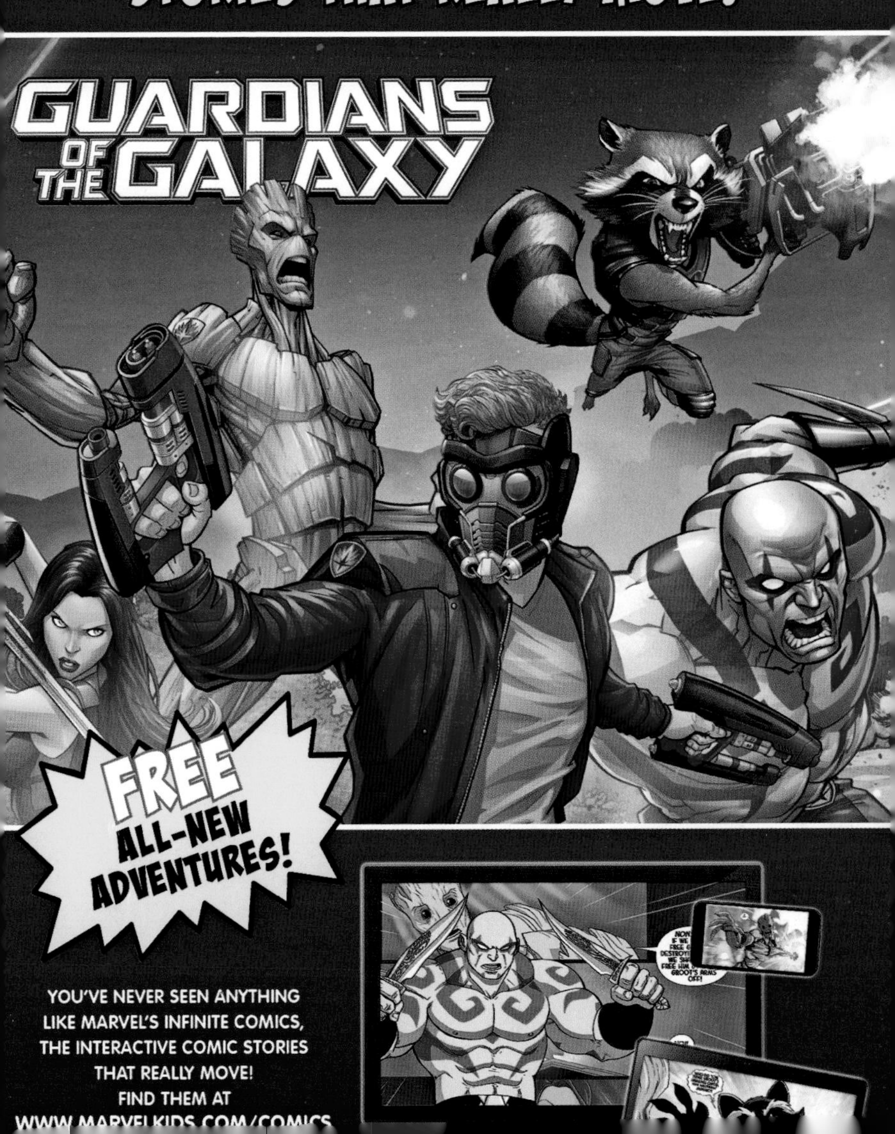
GUARDIANS OF THE GALAXY
FREE ALL-NEW ADVENTURES!
YOU'VE NEVER SEEN ANYTHING LIKE MARVEL'S INFINITE COMICS, THE INTERACTIVE COMIC STORIES THAT REALLY MOVE!
FIND THEM AT
WWW.MARVELKIDS.COM/COMICS

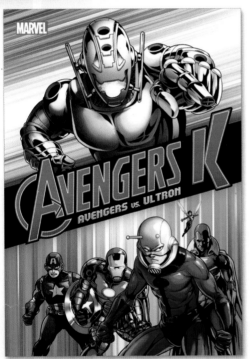